UNDER ONE FLAG

A Year at Rohwer

*To the teachers and administrators in the International Studies
magnet programs at Gibbs Elementary, Dunbar Middle School,
and Central High—with thanks.*
—LP

To my family—Suzanne, Mariah and Ian Clifton—with love.
—TC

Published 2005 by August House Publishers, Inc.
P.O. Box 3223, Little Rock, Arkansas, 72203,
501-372-5450
http://www.augusthouse.com

Printed in Korea by Pacifica Communications

10   9   8   7   6   5   4   3   2   1

Life Interrupted is a partnership between the University of Arkansas at Little Rock
Public History program and the Japanese American National Museum in
Los Angeles. Its mission is to research the experiences of Japanese Americans
in World War II Arkansas and educate the citizens of Arkansas and the nation
about the two camps at Jerome and Rohwer. Funding for the *Life Interrupted*
educational components, including this book, was provided by the Winthrop
Rockefeller Foundation. A portion of the proceeds from the sale of this book
will go toward the maintenance of the cemetery at Rohwer.

LIBRARY OF CONGRESS CATALOGING-IN-PUBLICATION DATA

Parkhurst, Liz Smith.
Under one flag : a year at Rohwer / by Liz Parkhurst ; illustrated by Tom Clifton.
p.   cm.
Summary: Based on historical events, Jeff, the son of an administrator at the War Relocation
Center in Rohwer, Arkansas, befriends George, a young Japanese American who is forced
to live in the camp with his family after his father is accused of being a spy.
ISBN 0-87483-759-6 (alk. paper)
1. Japanese Americans—Evacuation and relocation, 1942–1945—Juvenile fiction.
[1. Japanese Americans—Evacuation and relocation, 1942–1945—Fiction. 2. Friendship—
Fiction. 3. Race relations—Fiction. 4. World War, 1939–1945—United States—Fiction.
5. Arkansas—History—1933–1945—Fiction.]   I. Clifton, Tom, 1964– ill. II. Title.
PZ7.P23913Un   2005
[Fic]—dc22   2004046444

The paper used in this publication meets the minimum requirements
of the American National Standard for Information Sciences—
Permanence of Paper for Printed Library Materials, ANSI Z39.48-1984.

UNDER ONE FLAG

A Year at Rohwer

BY LIZ PARKHURST

ILLUSTRATED BY TOM CLIFTON

AUGUST HOUSE
Little folk

LITTLE ROCK

 hen I first woke up, I wasn't sure where I was. I sensed someone watching me from the side of the bed. When I turned my head, I didn't see my parents as I expected. I saw a boy about my age.

I blinked to be sure I was seeing correctly. I felt very groggy from the anesthesia still in my system. I remembered being rushed in to have my appendix removed. Because my father was an administrator at the War Relocation Center at Rohwer, the camp hospital was closest.

The boy, like most of the children residing in the prison camp, was dressed just as I dressed—that is, when I wasn't in the hospital.

"They keep checking to see if you're awake," he said.

"Who are you?" I tried to sit up, but gravity seemed to pull me down.

"I'm George," he said, extending his hand in greeting. "I'm a courier for the newspaper here in the camp—the *Rohwer Outpost.*" He held up a copy for my inspection. "What's your name?"

"Jefferson," I replied. "But everyone calls me Jeff—except my mama when she gets mad at me."

"I know what you mean. When my mother gets mad at me, she says my entire name: George Ichiro Kobayashi."

"You get in trouble, too?"

"I will in a minute if I don't deliver these papers to the nurses," he said. "I'm supposed to be working."

"Do you get paid?"

"Well, not really, but I get into lots of places where I wouldn't normally be allowed. I'm in here nearly every day, so I'll try to see you tomorrow."

Sure enough, George stopped by after school the next day. Mama had been visiting earlier and had left to go home and start dinner.

"Well, you didn't miss much at school," he said.

"Whose class are you in?" I asked.

"Miss Thompson's," he said. "She's not bad."

George was a year ahead of me. That was why I didn't recognize him.

"I'm in Miss Riley's class," I said. "It's tough because she's best friends with my aunt, so everything gets back to my parents."

George reached in his satchel and produced a small, decorated wooden box.

"Want to play marbles?"

"We aren't exactly outside in the dirt," I said. I was cranky and tired of being in bed.

That didn't stop George. "We can use this string that I have. See?" He took the string, made a circle on my bedcovers, and began dividing his marble collection for two players.

"You go first," he said.

But when I bent forward to line up my shot, I felt a sharp pain.

"My stitches," I winced. "I'd better not."

"OK," he said, "We can do this later—after you get your stitches out. There are other games we can play."

Five days later I was released. It was a breezy, balmy day—typical of March in the Arkansas Delta. George was waiting for me when I left the hospital. He was energetic and full of ideas.

"Let's make paper airplanes and see if we can fly them over the barracks."

Before the day was over, we had not only flown paper airplanes, we had made a model Eiffel Tower with paper and paste and used some gauze from the hospital to play Blind Man's Bluff.

It didn't take long to see why George knew so many people at Rohwer. He got along with everyone, adults and kids alike. My parents took to him right away, and soon we were spending most afternoons together after school.

Often we had to take George's younger sister, Nancy, along with us when their mother was working as a clerk in the dry goods department. Sometimes Daddy would give us permission to go to the little

general store just outside the camp. If we didn't have any luck, we would take Nancy to watch the older men carve the cypress knees gathered from the bayou nearby.

Baseball was one of our favorite pastimes. It was just as popular in the camp as it was in the rest of America. Our pick-up games grew popular as spring turned to summer. George was always near the top of the batting lineup, not so much because of his power but because of his speed. He could steal bases in broad daylight and slide into home plate like the greased pigs I chased in the contests at the county fair.

The day Dizzy Dean showed up was a day we would always remember. I don't mean the pitcher for the St. Louis Cardinals and the Chicago Cubs, although he did grow up in Arkansas, too. I mean the puppy who wandered in, skin and bones, and was soon wiggling in Nancy's arms. To tell the truth, the game pretty much fell apart after he showed up. It took all three of us to persuade my father to let the puppy stay in the camp. Mostly he stayed in our apartment, because pets weren't allowed in the inmates' barracks.

DIZZY DEAN SERVICE STATION

George and I also participated in the camp Boy Scout troop. We wore our uniforms proudly. We loved to march, even when it wasn't part of the program.

The troop gave George some time to be around grown men. When we first met, I had assumed his father was dead. I soon learned that he was being held in a Department of Justice detention center. Because he was a language teacher and spoke both English and Japanese, the U.S. authorities suspected he was a spy for the Japanese government.

"Men with badges came right after Pearl Harbor and took him away," George explained. "He's being held in New Mexico. He writes us letters. We write him. Nancy draws pictures for him."

At my insistence, my father began to help Mrs. Kobayashi in her efforts to get her husband released from the DOJ camp so that he could join his family at Rohwer. Daddy wrote some letters on behalf of the Kobayashi family. My grandfather had long known U.S. Senator Hattie Caraway, and she was able to open some doors for him.

We spent all spring practicing our Scout skills and working on merit badges. We studied Morse code: three longs, three shorts, and three longs meant "S.O.S."—"We're in trouble." We memorized the flag signals used between ships to communicate during radio blackouts. Our favorite activity was knot-tying—bowlines, double half-hitches, the more complicated the better.

In June the troop participated in a jamboree in Mississippi, a weeklong campout with Scouts from three states. We competed with the other troops for prizes.

The first aid contest was the most fun. We tied "broken" legs to splints; treated "patients" for shock; and carried "wounded" on stretchers to the first aid station. Our troop came in second in the compass contest—orienteering, we called it. It was set up like a treasure hunt with prizes hidden at the end of each location drill.

Food always seems to taste better when you eat outdoors, and we looked forward to supper every night. We were usually worn out from a full day of activities, and the hot food seemed like a reward for a hard day's work. We cooked potatoes in the hot coals of our campfire and baked pot pies in the tin-foil ovens we devised.

The day before Thanksgiving, my parents and I prepared to visit my grandparents at their farm near Monticello. We would spend five days with them. When I brought my suitcase from the apartment, Daddy and Mama stood next to the car, beaming. Inside the car were George, Nancy, and Mrs. Kobayashi. They were going to spend the day with us. We were even taking Dizzy Dean. My Thanksgiving would be complete.

I hardly recognized Nancy, the little tomboy who caught turtles and lizards with us. She wore a neatly pressed dress and freshly polished maryjanes. In her hair she wore a hand-painted comb, just as her mother did.

George and his family, like many of the inmates, were not fond of Southern cooking. Seated at my grandparents' table, they bypassed the greens and other vegetables, which were overcooked for their taste. They politely tasted the turkey but filled up mostly on Grandma's biscuits.

"How can you not like grits and black-eyed peas?" I asked. "You don't know what you're missing."

Mama hushed me, afraid I would embarrass them in front of my family. She needn't have worried. George surprised us all by accepting my grandfather's dare to eat the "rare delicacy" that he offered him. George laughed harder than anyone when Grandpa told him that the delicacy was venison.

"Lord have mercy, Harold," my grandmother scolded. "Jeff's friends are going to think we're some kind of country yokels."

"No, Mae," he laughed. "We just come from good old pioneer stock."

The week after Thanksgiving, I woke to a banging on my bedroom window. I knew it was George. He had long ago quit using the front door. Sleepily, I raised the window. I was no match for George's energy—he was wide awake and beaming. He wiggled through the window and into my room.

"Good news!" he shouted.

"Well, I can see that," I said. "What is it?"

"My father is coming! He'll be here in time for Christmas!"

He picked up Dizzy Dean and danced around the room singing: *"Mairzy dotes and dozy dotes and little lamsy divey / A kiddly divey too, wooden you? ..."*

He collapsed in laughter. Then, for the first time, I sensed how sad he had been all this time and how hard he had worked to cover it up.

"Are you nervous?" I asked.

"A little. I haven't seen him in nearly a year."

"What is he like?"

"He's the best dad ever. All my friends back in California liked him. So did his students. We just don't understand how the government could have thought he was dangerous."

"It doesn't seem fair, that someone who is so well-respected would be taken away as a prisoner of war."

"Oh, my mother and I have talked about that many times. What are they afraid he might do, attack someone with a book?"

I looked at him seriously for a few seconds, and then we both started to laugh. Soon we were chattering like always, making plans for the holidays and his father's return.

Three days before Christmas, George, Nancy, and Mrs. Kobayashi stood near the entrance of the camp. They were waiting for George's father to arrive on the train. I watched from several yards away. When he stepped off the train, Mrs. Kobayashi started toward him, but George and Nancy ran to him first. Soon they were all hugging each other.

Over the next few days, I did not see George very much. He spent his time showing his father around the camp and introducing him to as many people as he could, especially to the other Japanese American boys. George's parents did pay a call on mine, but it was a short visit and a bit formal, as grownups can be. George and Nancy were at home making Christmas presents, Mrs. Kobayashi said, and I kept thinking how much livelier the visit would be if they had come along.

With George and Nancy occupied with their father, our apartment was very quiet during the holidays. But I was glad George had his father back. I tried to imagine what it would be like to be separated from my father, but I couldn't. I was happy for George that all of his family was together again.

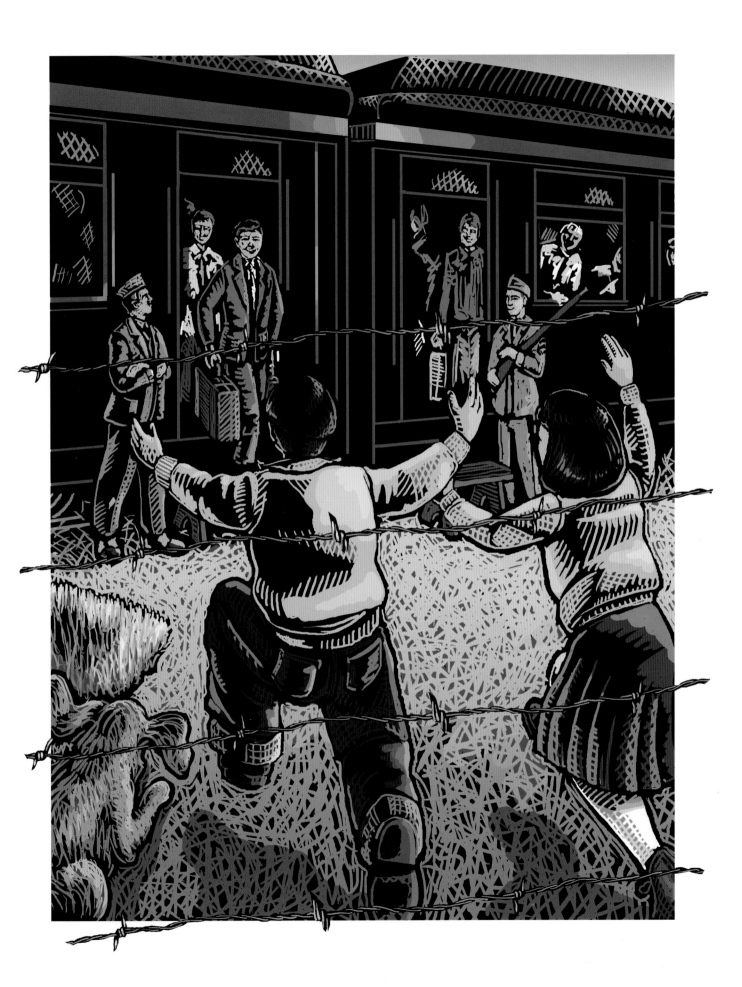

After the New Year, George's father began to teach Japanese language classes in the camp. My parents let me take the class. I thought it would be full of administrators and teachers from the camp, but many Japanese Americans—my parents' age as well as my age—were in the class as well. When class was over, I asked George about that.

"We are three generations," he explained. "The elders, the Issei, are the first generation to immigrate to the U.S. from Japan. Japanese is their first language, and most of them know little English.

"Both of my parents are Nisei, the first to be born American citizens. Most of them grew up speaking both languages but dropped the Japanese outside of their homes. And I am Sansei, the next generation yet. I probably wouldn't know any Japanese if my father wasn't a language teacher."

Arkansas in the winter ranges from shirtsleeve weather to freezing temperatures. The spell we had been having lately was no fun at all—cold, damp, and overcast. It felt good to snuggle under the covers, and I was never in a hurry to get out of bed. So I thought I was dreaming when I heard the banging at my window one Saturday morning in February.

"Jeff, get out of bed!" George shouted.

I groaned and crawled further under the pile of blankets.

"There's a magic fairy land in Rohwer!" Nancy called from behind him. "You must come outside now. Immediately."

"This is no fairy land," George argued with her. "We're in the land of the snow forts. We have been transported to the German front."

Snow? I sat up immediately.

We got snow rarely in south Arkansas—maybe every three or four winters. George and Nancy, on the other hand, had never seen snow before. They had grown up in southern California, after all. They ran off, shouting to the other kids and bending down to roll snowballs. Dizzy Dean walked gingerly on the snow, sinking through it in confusion and leaving tracks on the glossy surface.

By the time I was bundled up to Mama's satisfaction, every block in the camp had formed a troop. Each brigade built its own snow fort and formed a snowball manufacturing unit. George made an effort to get us organized.

"We're the Brits," he yelled to the kids from another block. "You guys be the Germans."

"No! You can be the Germans!"

An argument ensued, and I never was sure who threw the first snowball. But after that, chaos erupted, and it was everyone for himself. We fought the entire day and never ran out of snow or energy.

Three weeks later, all evidence of the snow was gone. The temperatures were in the 50s, and the sun and wind shot through the bare trees. School was out for a few days, and I wandered around looking for George. We had planned to start baseball practice during the school break.

I saw him emerge from the camp office. I assumed he had been on a delivery, but then his parents and sister stepped out behind him. Then my father stepped out. He spoke to Mr. Kobayashi and shook his hand.

George spoke quietly to his parents for a minute, and they nodded and stepped back. As he approached me, he had a strange look on his face. I couldn't tell if he was happy or sad.

"My father has found a teaching job," he said. "We're going to be allowed to move to Colorado. He's going to be at the U.S. Navy Japanese Language School."

Mr. Kobayashi had been recruited by the U.S. government to teach the naval officers-in-training to speak and understand Japanese. George and his family would be leaving in April.

"Hey, Dad, is the school open?" George asked his father. "I want to look Boulder up on the map."

"It should be, I know some of the teachers are trying to get caught up on their paperwork."

We ran to the classroom where the big jigsaw puzzle of the United States was assembled. George found Colorado right away.

"There it is, see?" he said. "It's out of the exclusion zone." He pointed to the Pacific Coast and southwest Arizona. "None of us can go back there. But Boulder, Colorado, is in the clear!"

I went home and cried for a very long time. It was wonderful news for the Kobayashi family. They would once again live in freedom. But I would be losing my best friend. Dizzy Dean nuzzled me, and I reached down and scratched his ears.

Then it struck me. What would we do about Dizzy Dean? He belonged to all of us. I jumped up and ran to the Kobayashis' barracks. George answered the door.

"Are you allowed to have dogs in Colorado?" I asked.

He laughed. "If I managed to keep one in a prison camp, I can probably manage one on the outside."

But Mr. Kobayashi spoke up. "George, there is no way the government is going to allow a dog on the train, with security being so high."

"We could hide him," George said.

"A dog that big and energetic?" his father said. "Sorry, son, you're going to have to leave him in Jeff's hands."

I loved that dog, but even so I wanted George to take him. The Kobayashis would be starting over with nothing from their original home, only the few things they had been allowed to bring to Rohwer. He could use something friendly and familiar in a strange, faraway place.

Weeks later, my parents and I stood at the same train stop where I had watched George greet his father at Christmastime. Now they would travel up the opposite track, away from the scene of so many adventures.

"Well, at least you managed to avoid another Arkansas summer," my father joked to Mr. Kobayashi. "Although you will have your fill of snow next winter."

"Well, if we do, we can come back here to visit," Mr. Kobayashi said.

"Right," George grinned. "Just in time for spring training." He stuffed his baseball glove inside his knapsack, shook my hand, and boarded the train.

It has been more than sixty years since that year that George and I spent together as boys. The move to Boulder wasn't all that easy for his family. I could not believe that a woman as smart and organized as Mrs. Kobayashi could not find a job. She had many interviews that she thought went well, but no one ever called to offer her work.

There were other slights as well, but George didn't seem to want to say much about them. When we were in our teens, he came to resent the way the government had treated the Japanese Americans during the war, as well as the prejudice they faced for a long time after.

Because they had lost everything in the relocation process, the Kobayashis had little savings. While my parents could send me to the university in Fayetteville, George had to work for a couple of years after high school to save for college, and even then, he held two jobs while he went to school. He was so busy during those years that we just lost touch.

The farm near Monticello that used to be my grandparents' is mine now. It's not unusual for Japanese Americans to come by our house, since we still live near Rohwer and folks around here know I lived in the camp. I usually stop what I'm doing and spend some time talking to the visitors. I figure they didn't ask to be locked up, and the least I can do is help them connect to their past.

One day, as I was on my tractor, I looked up to see my wife greeting a Japanese American family on the front porch of our home. I went to greet them. As I got off the tractor, my dog trailed behind me.

"He kind of reminds me of a dog I used to have," said the grandfather as he stepped toward me. "He went by the name of Dizzy Dean."

★

During World War II, nearly 120,000 Americans of Japanese ancestry were imprisoned in War Relocation Centers by the U.S. government even though they were guilty of no crimes. Fear and wartime hysteria led President Franklin D. Roosevelt to sign Executive Order 9066, which effectively forced Japanese and Japanese Americans from their homes on the West Coast of the United States. Many families, like the Kobayashis in this story, were separated during the war. Respected community members, due to their ties with Japan and Japanese culture, were rounded up and taken for questioning by the FBI in the days and months immediately following the Japanese attack on Pearl Harbor.

More than 8,000 such citizens were taken by train to Rohwer, Arkansas, one of two War Relocation Centers in Arkansas. By 1942, a compound of tarpaper and wooden barracks had sprung up in the Arkansas Delta, behind barbed wire and in the shadow of guard towers. Abandoning homes, businesses, and jobs, the prisoners were allowed to bring only what they could carry to the prison camps. Family pets had to be given away or left in the care of friends. Occasionally, however, stray animals, such as Dizzy Dean in this story, appeared in camp and were cared for by the inmates.

Administrators, teachers, and military police also lived in the camps where they worked. A few, like Jeff's father, chose to bring their families to live in the sheetrocked apartments inside the camps. Inside Rohwer, children attended school, ate meals in the mess halls, and participated in Scouting and sporting events. As the war progressed and it became evident that the inmates at Rohwer posed no security risk, they were sometimes allowed to leave the camp to visit the nearby general store or travel to Pine Bluff or Little Rock.

Families who received job offers outside the exclusion zone (the Pacific Coast and southwest Arizona) could apply to leave the camps. Many former inmates, like Mr. Kobayashi, served their country by joining the military or working for the government. In 1945, the military exclusion order was lifted, and the prisoners returned to the West Coast or moved elsewhere to begin the difficult task of starting their lives over. More than four decades later, in 1988, the U.S. government formally apologized to the Japanese Americans.

In the Arkansas Delta, little remains today of the prison camps at Rohwer and Jerome. A cemetery still stands at Rohwer today. Twenty-five Japanese American gravesites and two monuments serve as a reminder of this bleak period in U.S. history. A portion of the proceeds from the sale of this book funds the maintenance and upkeep of this cemetery.

—KRISTIN DUTCHER MANN
Assistant Professor of History and Social Studies Education
University of Arkansas at Little Rock

More information about the camps at Rohwer and Jerome
can be found on the Life Interrupted website at
http://www.lifeinterrupted.org.